You Read to Me, I'll Read to You

Very Short Tall Tales to Read Together

By

MARY ANN HOBERMAN

Illustrated by

MICHAEL EMBERLEY

Megan Tingley Books

LITTLE, BROWN AND COMPANY

New York   Boston

To Megan Tingley,
gifted editor and cherished friend
—M.A.H.

To Saho,
for all the patience, skill, kindness, and respect,
designing this and so many other books
—M.E.

The illustrations for this book were done in pencil, watercolor, and dry pastel on 90-pound hot-pressed watercolor paper. This book was edited by Megan Tingley and designed by Saho Fujii under the art direction of Patti Ann Harris. The production was supervised by Erika Schwartz, and the production editor was Barbara Bakowski. The text and the display type were set in Shannon.

Table Of Contents

Author's Note:

The tall tale is a unique form of American storytelling. Its heroes and heroines are larger than life, and their deeds are amazing. Some of these characters were actual people, while others were created out of whole cloth. In all the tales, exaggeration is primary, the more the better! And in their repeated tellings over the years, they have become an important part of our American literature.

These rhyming stories, like all the others in the YOU READ TO ME, I'LL READ TO YOU series, are written for two voices. The readers can be either beginners or more advanced, or they can be a combination of the two. They may be young or old or one of each. And, of course, the stories are also fun to do as choral readings, with any number of participants.

The original idea for these books grew out of my work with Literacy Volunteers of America, now known as ProLiteracy, an organization dedicated to encouraging literacy and the joy of reading throughout the world. And in this newest addition to the series, the fun of reading is first and foremost!

Introduction

This book is full of funny tales
That are both short and tall.

>Both short and tall at once, you say?
>I don't get that at all.

They're short because they are not long.

>Well, that is plain to see;
>But how can they be tall as well?
>Explain that part to me.

Tall tales tell tales of times gone by
With heroes strong and great
Who did things you might not believe.
Tall tales exaggerate.

>But did these heroes really live?

Some of them did, not all.
Sometimes the deeds they did are real;
But sometimes they are tall.

>So tall can have two meanings.
>Not true is also tall.
>I'll read to you, you'll read to me,
>Until we've read them all.

Annie Oakley

Annie Oakley, what a shot!
She could hit most any spot!
In a contest with a gun,
Bet your britches Annie won!

> When she was a little kid,
> She learned shooting, Annie did.
> Shot to keep her family fed.
> Had to do it, Annie said.

Not long after, she went west,
Showed them all she was the best.
While some guys were pretty good,
They couldn't shoot like Annie could.

> Once a fellow nearly tied;
> But Annie beat him, though he tried.
> And then what happened? Can you guess?

He fell in love with Annie, yes!

> And Annie felt the very same.
> Frank E. Butler was his name.
> So Frank and Annie tied the knot,

But Annie was the better shot.

> Frank didn't mind, he loved her so.
> He helped her in the Wild West Show.
> They toured in lands both near and far,
> And Annie Oakley was the star.

From ninety feet Frank tossed a dime,
And Annie shot it down each time.
From ninety feet she'd even get
The ash off of his cigarette;

**And never did she ever miss.
(Can you imagine doing this?)**

Sitting Bull was struck with awe,
Was amazed at what he saw,
Made her an adopted Sioux,
Named her "Little Sure Shot," too.

In Germany (this is a fact)
The kaiser came to see her act;
But when he asked her at her show
To try the ash trick, she said no.

"Not in your mouth," she firmly said.
"Please hold it in your hand instead."

**(Although she never missed a thing,
Imagine if she killed a king!)**

Annie Oakley's fame has grown.
Annie's name is widely known.
So are her tales, both tall and true.
You read to me, I'll read to you.

Davy Crockett

I'm Davy Crockett, frontier king,
A man who can do anything.
My story starts right at my birth:
A comet carried me to Earth.
It hit a hill in Tennessee,
And guess what happened? Out came me!

    That's quite a story, if it's true.
    Now let me hear what you can do.

Well, here's a tale that's often told:
When I was only three years old,
A bear snuck in to steal some jam.
(And this will show how strong I am!)
I squeezed that bear, so big and brown,
And squeezed and squeezed till he fell down.

    That's mighty fine, I do agree.
    That's mighty fine for only three.

A few years later, two or three,
My pa gave my first gun to me.
I named it Betsy, just for fun.

    You sure were young to own a gun.
    Why did your father give you one?

Back then we had to hunt for meat.
Without our guns, we wouldn't eat.

    So you learned how to shoot?

Yes, sir!
Of all the shots that ever were,
I was the sharpest and the best,
The champion of both east and west;
And all the critters knew it, too.
So when I came, guess what they'd do?

    They'd run away?

No, they would not.
They'd just give up without a shot.
They'd each surrender, all at once.
Those critters kept us fed for months.

    The tallest tale you ever spun
    Was how you once unfroze the sun.

One icy day of winds and snows
The sunlight froze before it rose.
The night went on and on. No dawn.
It looked as if the day was gone.

    What had happened? What was wrong?

The reason that the night was long
Was that the Earth was frozen stuck
And couldn't turn.

    What rotten luck!

The poor old sun was frozen, too.
And stuck in ice.

    What did you do?

I took some bear grease, half a ton,
And poured it out upon the sun,
Which soon began to blaze and burn;
And then the Earth began to turn.

    So we all owe our lives to you?

Well, not to brag, but so you do.

Davy Crockett's tales are mixed—
Parts are tall and parts are true;
But either one, they all are fun!
You read to me, I'll read to you!

John Henry

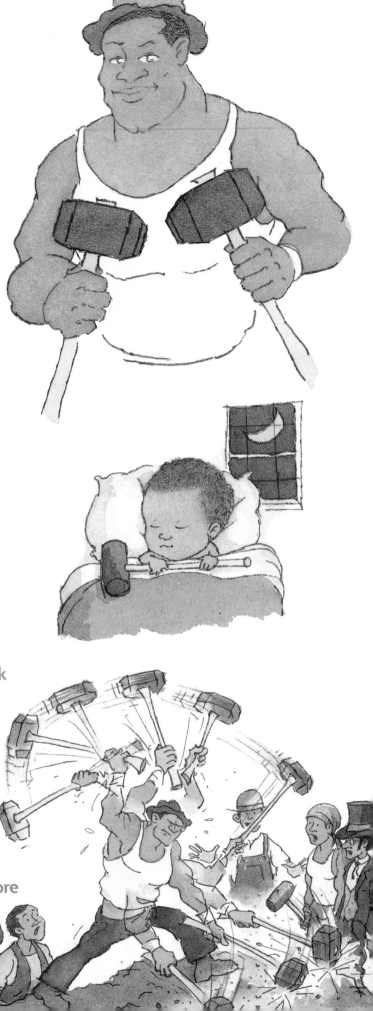

John Henry was a man of steel,
A great steel-driving man.
Folks said, "No one in all the world
Can do the things he can."

    The very night that he was born,
    The sky was black as coal.
    The people trembled in their beds
    To hear the thunder roll.

The baby who was born that night
Was sturdy as an ox,
With legs as thick as tree trunks
And arms as hard as rocks.

    They wondered who this baby was
    And how he came and why;
    But when John Henry gave a smile,
    It lit up all the sky.

And most remarkable of all,
Though hard to understand,
John Henry held, when he was born,
A hammer in his hand!

    He carried stones for railroad gangs
    The year that he was five;
    And from the start he did more work
    Than any child alive.

At ten he started hammering;
He drove spikes all day long;
And as he hammered through the rock,
He sang his steel-man song.

    The bosses brought a steam-drill in.
    It did the work of ten.
    They said there'd be no need no more
    For any driving men.

John Henry thought about his son
And Polly Ann, his wife.
He needed work to care for them
And driving was his life.

> "I do the work of twenty men,"
> The great John Henry said.
> "If I can't beat that new machine,
> I'd rather I was dead."

They organized a contest—
Man against machine—
A contest that in all the world
Had never yet been seen.

The drill machine, it led at first;
It drove steel twice as fast.
John Henry grabbed two hammers
And pulled ahead at last.

> And then the drill machine broke down!
> John Henry, he had won!
> But still he kept on hammering
> To get the tunnel done.

But he had strained so hard and long
To break the rock apart,
His arms and legs no longer worked,
Nor did his mighty heart.

> They carried great John Henry home.
> They laid him down to rest
> Beside the house where he was born,
> The place he loved the best.

John Henry's tale of derring-do,
It may be tall, it may be true;
But true or tall, we like it all.
You read to me, I'll read to you.

Slue-Foot Sue and Pecos Bill

I'm Slue-Foot Sue.
I was the bride
Of Pecos Bill,
And I could ride!

    Oh, yes, you could,
    My darling Sue!
    That's why I fell
    In love with you.

A catfish swam
At my command.
I rode it down
The Rio Grande.

    I spied you there
    And made a wish
    To meet the rider
    Of that fish!

You courted me
Both night and day.
You even shot
The stars away!

    I shot them all
    Except for one,
    Just one remained
    When I was done.

Now Texas is
The Lone Star State
Because of me!
I think that's great!

I had a horse
No one could tame.
Widow Maker
Was his name.

That horse was reckless,
Wild and free.
No one could ride that horse
But me.

Before I'd marry you,
Of course,
I said I had to
Ride your horse.

You had a bustle
On your gown.
You started bouncing
Up and down.

Your bronco bucked!
He bumped me high!
He bucked and bumped me
To the sky!

You hit the moon!
What could I do?
I saved you
With my snake lasso.

That rattlesnake,
It saved my life;
And that's when I
Became your wife.

We're Pecos Bill
And Slue-Foot Sue.
Our tales are tall.
Our tales are true.
They started small
And then they grew.
You read to me.
I'll read to you.

Febold Feboldson

I'll tell you of a famous Swede
Called Febold Feboldson,
A lonely farmer on the plains,
The one and only one.

> Each time some Forty-Niners passed,
> He'd yell, "Come plant a crop!"
> But they were heading west for gold,
> And none of them would stop.

He bought ten thousand goldfish
And dropped them in his lake.
The fish looked just like gold, of course.
(Of course, the gold was fake!)

> The next train saw the golden lake
> And raced back to the spot,
> Believing that the lake was gold—
> But then the day grew hot.

The dusty winds began to blow;
The weather started turning.
The folks all jumped into the lake
To save themselves from burning!

> But when they saw how they'd been fooled,
> They ran back to their train.
> "Don't go!" yelled Febold after them.
> "I promise it will rain!"

Febold put on his thinking cap
And tried another caper.
He built a giant fire,
Which turned the lake to vapor.

> The vapor changed to clouds, then rain,
> Which followed Febold's scheme.
> But since the weather was so hot,
> The rain soon turned to steam.

And when the steam turned into fog,
The crowd began to cuss.
"We can't see anything at all!
This place is not for us!"

The crowd once more packed up their gear.
Febold sank to his knees.
"Just give me one more chance!" he begged.
"Oh please, oh please, oh please!

"Think of July the Fourth," he said,
"And how it always rains.
The fireworks make lots of noise
And everyone complains.

"It's noise that makes the rains come down,
So all we have to do
Is figure out how we can make
A great hullabaloo!"

Febold said, "Frogs make lots of noise,
So here's my latest hunch:
I bet that we can make it rain
If we just catch a bunch."

They all went out and caught some frogs.
The frogs, they started croaking;
And suddenly the rains came down!
Old Febold wasn't joking!

And soon those Forty-Niners
Were farmers, yes, siree!
I'll read their tale again to you.
You'll read it back to me.

Johnny Appleseed

Who's that fellow over there?
His clothes are torn. His feet are bare.
He wears a saucepan for a hat.
I've never seen a hat like that.
Tell me, mister, who you are
And have you come from very far?

I've come from Massachusetts, yes,
That's pretty far away, I guess.

Well, you're in Indiana now,
Walking barefoot! Tell me how
And why you've come and what you do.
I've never seen a man like you.

When I was young and lived at home,
I'd often leave our house and roam.
My parents had ten girls and boys.
I'd go off to escape their noise.

Where did you go to get away?

I went out to the woods to play.
I got to know each plant and tree
And I decided what to be.

What did you think? What was your plan?

I thought I'd be an apple man.

An apple man? Explain that, please.

A person who plants apple trees.
I get my seeds from cider mills
And wander through the dales and hills,
Planting seeds each place I go
And watching all my orchards grow.

With all the orchards that you've made
And all your work, do you get paid?

The bees work hard and work for free.
It is the very same with me.
I plant my seeds and sing my song.
I don't need much to get along,
And what I get, I always spend
To help old, ailing horses mend
And every person is my friend.

Well, you're a wonder, yes, indeed!
Just think of all the folks you feed!
I sure am happy that you came.
And by the way, what is your name?

It once was Chapman, first name John.
Not anymore. My old name's gone.
Each place I go, they've all agreed
To call me Johnny Appleseed!

Appleseed! That name is nice!
Now when folks eat an apple slice,
They'll think of Johnny as they chew!
You read to me, I'll read to you!

Alfred Bulltop Stormalong

I'm Alfred Bulltop Stormalong.
I am a sailor big and strong.
I am a sailor tough and tall.
I am the greatest gob of all.

> Now let me get your story straight.
> What makes you think you are so great?

Well, you just take a look at me,
The biggest sailor on the sea.
I stand eight fathoms high, I do.
That's fifty feet to folks like you.

> Why, I should think at fifty feet
> With you aboard, you'd sink the fleet!

I started as a cabin boy.
The captain shouted, "Ship ahoy!
Help hoist the anchor, Stormalong!"
We all pulled hard, but things went wrong.

> What was the matter?

Worst of luck!
We couldn't move! The anchor stuck!

> What did you do to free your boat?

Took off my pants, my hat and coat,
My shoes and socks, then took a leap
Straight down into the briny deep.

> Why were you stuck? What did you find?

I found an octopus entwined,
A slimy two-ton octopus.
That beast would not let go of us.

> I would have swum away!

Not me!
I pulled that eight-armed creature free.
I wrestled it into a knot
And tied it up right on the spot.

Well, Stormalong, that's quite a tale!
And after that, where did you sail?

Before I took another trip,
I grew too big to fit the ship.
I thought I'd try dry land instead,
So I went west to earn my bread.

Where did you go? What western state?

I went to Kansas. It was great.
I grew potatoes. Got all set.
(I kept them watered with my sweat.)

What brought you back to port once more?

I tired of my life ashore.
I missed the sea, the salty brine.
I saw the sailor's life was mine.

Where did you find a ship to fit?

My sailor pals constructed it,
The biggest ship that's sailed the Earth.
A block-long hammock is my berth.
My ship has masts that stretch so high,
They punch deep holes into the sky.

A ship and sailor of such size,
As tall tales go, this takes the prize!
But whether it is tall or true,
You read to me, I'll read to you.

Mose the Fireman

Long ago in old New York,
A man named Mose loved beans and pork;
But even more, without a doubt,
Old Mose loved putting fires out.

Eight feet tall, with hair of red,
A stovepipe hat upon his head,
That hat made him look ten feet tall,
The biggest fireman of all.

One day, as Mose sat down to eat,
He heard a shout from down the street.
"Fire! Fire! Don't delay!
Firefighters! On your way!"

Mose went dashing off in haste.
To the firehouse he raced.
All his men were in the yard
With their pumper, pulling hard.

Down the avenues they ran
With the pumper. Every man
Racing fast with pounding feet
Till something stopped them in the street.

The way was blocked for, worst of luck,
A horse-drawn trolley stood there, stuck!
"Her wheel is caught," the driver cried.
"My nags can't move her, though they've tried."

Mose took a puff of his cigar
And lifted up the trolley car.
They pulled the pump across the track,
And then Mose put the trolley back.

By now the fire burned so high,
It lit up the entire sky.
"Let's get going, men!" Mose said,
And off the firefighters sped.

Then suddenly a woman's shout!
"Will someone get my baby out?
She's three floors up!" they hear her cry.
"Oh, save her, sirs, or she will die!"

The firefighters huff and puff.
Their ladder's not quite tall enough.
What can they do? Says Mose, "Don't fret!
Bend over, Bob! Bend over, Brett!
We'll put the ladder on your backs!"

Old Mose climbs up and takes his ax
And chops the window big and wide
So his great bulk can fit inside.

By now the flames are pouring out!
Old Mose is dead! There's not a doubt.
And then the ladder starts to burn.
Old Mose is gone. He won't return.

But look! There's Mose! He takes a jump
And lands with a tremendous thump!
He's black with soot! And look at that:
His head is bare. Where is his hat?

"Oh, where's my baby? Where's my child?"
The woman screams. Her eyes are wild!
Mose shows his hat. They crowd around
And see the baby, safe and sound!

They pull the pumper back through town
And dry it off and put it down;
And Mose, after he scrubs and cleans,
Goes back to eat his pork and beans.

That's quite a story, we agree.
I'll read to you, you'll read to me.

21

Mike Fink

I am Mike Fink, the keelboat boss!
No wrestler can defeat me!
The only time I lost a fight,
I beat the guy who beat me!

> You hardly learned to read or write.
> You didn't have much schooling.
> If you had done just half your brags,
> I'd still think you were fooling.

I wasn't even one year old
First time I ran away.
They caught me, but I showed them all.
I left again next day.

> That tale's a bunch of hogwash!
> It's just some crazy talk!
> To run away before you're one?
> You couldn't even walk!

You telling me what I could do?
Well, take another think!
Nobody in the whole wide world
Can contradict Mike Fink!

> Come on, Mike Fink, don't talk so tough.
> Calm down and rest a minute.
> You had a fight with Keelboat Jack.
> I heard you didn't win it.

Aw, I was just a kid back then.
It was a stupid tussle.
So I went wrestling grizzly bears
And put on lots of muscle.
Then I went back to Keelboat Jack
And made another dare;
And when we wrestled one more time,
I beat him fair and square.

Well, you're a bragger, sure enough!
There's never been your like!
Of all the braggers in the world,
The braggingest is Mike!

I'll say I am! I am the best!
Don't care if tongues are wagging!
In everything I am the king,
And that includes my bragging!

I know you're strong as iron,
But Bunyan, he was, too;
And while you're good at shooting,
Davy Crockett's good as you.

But I caught alligators
And I knocked them for a loop,
And wrestled snapping turtles
And boiled them for my soup.

But you were finally beat, Mike Fink,
Years after you began.

Yes, I admit I was brought down,
But not by any man.

And not by any animal,
Nor enemy nor friend.
Those smoky, noisy, dirty steamboats
Beat you in the end.

And that part of the story,
While very sad, is true.
You read to me about it,
And then I'll read to you.

Sally Ann Thunder Ann Whirlwind

Look at that lady, so tall and so strong!
Her arms are so big, and her legs are so long!
I've never seen anyone looking like her.

    I'm Sally Ann Thunder Ann Whirlwind, yes, sir.

Where do you come from, Miss Sally Ann Thunder?

    I come from the mountains, and I am a wonder.
    The day I was born I could talk, yes, I could.

Talk on your first day? Say, that's pretty good.

    And not only talk. From my birth, I could run.

Run on your first day?

    Yes, sir, from day one.
    I'd nine older brothers who mocked me with scorn.
    I outran them all from the day I was born.

I bet they were angry. I bet they were mad.
Beat by a baby. That sounds pretty bad.

    At first they were jealous. They never could win.
    But then they grew proud because I was their kin.

And when you got older, well, what happened then?

    I left for the forest to live far from men.
    I lived with the animals, passed all my days
    Learning their secrets and watching their ways.

Did you ever get scared in your life, Sally Ann?

> Only one time, by a beast, not a man.
> One icy, cold winter I hid in a lair,
> And all of a sudden, why, there was a bear,
> Angry and hungry and ready to eat,
> Ready to eat me, a nice chunk of meat.

Oh, Sally Ann Thunder Ann, what did you do?

> I laughed in his face, and my grin grew and grew.
> My grin grew so wide and so big and so bright,
> It clear knocked him over! Oh, that was a sight!

Well, you are a wonder, for sure, Sally Ann!
You're pretty, you're smart, and you're strong as a man!
Do you have a boyfriend?

> Why, yes, sir, I do.
> His name's Davy Crockett.

Is that really true?

> I rescued him when he was stuck in a tree.
> I tied up ten rattlesnakes, yanking him free.
> I looked in his eyes, and that minute I knew,
> And Davy fell crazy in love with me, too.

And did you get married, Davy and you?

> We sure did get married. We both said, "I do."

We settled down happily—everyone knows,
Raised up a family, and that's how it goes,
Wrote down our tales for our children to see.
Now I'm reading to them, and they're reading to me.

Paul Bunyan

I'm the mighty Paul Bunyan,
Best logger of all.
When I bellow, "Timber!"
Then twenty trees fall!

> You've got to be lying!
> That cannot be done!
> You cannot cut twenty
> At once, only one.

Not when you're Paul Bunyan!
I swing my ax round,
And twenty tall pine trees
All fall to the ground.

> I do not believe you!
> Your story's too weird!

Well, how do you think
All the prairies got cleared?

> You're claiming you cleared them?
> You're claiming that, too?

I am, and that's not all
Paul Bunyan can do.
I dug the Grand Canyon.

> Now that tale's too tall!
> You dug the Grand Canyon?
> You've gone too far, Paul!

Not when you're a giant
The day you are born.
Ten storks had to bring me
That Maine winter morn.

> Ten storks for one baby?

Ten storks brought me there.
My weight set a record—
One hundred pounds bare!

26

Your tales are impossible,
Worse than I feared.

And what's better yet,
I was born with a beard!
A bushy black beard
That they combed with a rake.

A beard on a baby?
Well, that takes the cake!

Then when I was twenty,
The snow came down blue.
I heard someone crying.

So what did you do?

I dug in a snowdrift,
Through ice and through rocks,
And guess what I found there?
A blue baby ox!

Your stories grow stranger.
An ox that was blue?

A blue ox named Babe,
And he grew and he grew.
And now we're best buddies.
We've logged near and far.
Wherever there's timber
To fell, there we are!

Your tales are amazing,
As tall as a tree!
I'll read them to you,
And you'll read them to me!

The Great Don Jose Love-Mad Lopez

Don Jose Lopez am I,
The Great Jose Lopez!
Love-Mad Lopez I'm also called!
Three different names, oh, yes!

      But why do you have all those names?
      Most folk get by with one.

Why, I'm too great for just one name!
I'll tell you all I've done.
Now first of all, you probably think
I travel on a horse,
The way that other people do.

      Why, yes, I do, of course.

Well, you are wrong, amigo,
As wrong as you can be!
I ride upon a flying palm!

      You ride a flying tree?

Indeed I do. I jump aboard
And rise into the sky
And rescue ladies in distress;
And then away we fly!

      Well, that explains why you are called
      Love-Mad Lopez, it's clear.
      What other deeds, Don, have you done
      Throughout your long career?

I taught coyotes how to sing.
I hushed their noisy cries.

      You taught coyotes how to sing?

And also harmonize.
I dug out San Francisco Bay.

      Why, that is really fine.

And also the Grand Canyon.

Now there I draw the line!

They say Paul Bunyan did it. No!
'Twas I, the very one!
They give Paul Bunyan credit
For deeds that I have done.

Paul Bunyan cut down lots of trees.

With me it was reversed.
I planted trees, not cut them down!
The redwoods were the first.
And though I am a modest man
And do not like to boast,
I settled California,
Right up and down the coast.

Well, if you say so, Don Jose.

You do not claim to doubt me?
The West would never have been won
Or looked so good without me!
Now adios, amigo.
I'm rising from the ground
Upon my flying palm tree
On new adventures bound.

The Love-Mad Don Jose Lopez,
His stories grew and grew!
You read me one. It will be fun.
And I'll read one to you.

Casey Jones

I'm Casey Jones, the engineer.
In songs and stories I appear.
I drove a train, you may recall.

       And I'm his engine, Cannonball.

You and I were quite a pair.
No train went faster anywhere.
Not a hill we couldn't climb,
And we were always right on time.

       You and I, we sure had fun
       Each time we took the Memphis run,
       Rolling down to New Orleans.

Yep, we sure were full of beans!

       I'd pull my trainload back and forth
       Heading south, then heading north;
       And everything was mighty fine
       As we went speeding down the line.

One April day we had to wait.
We started off two hours late;
But since the day was clear and bright
And since our load was pretty light,
I thought before this day is done
I bet we'll set a record run.

We left the station, picked up speed.
Full throttle now, we both agreed.

I huffed and puffed, began to climb.
I knew we could make up the time.

We reach the mountaintop at last.
It's downhill now. We're going fast.

Five minutes late, a bit behind.
We'll make it up, so never mind.

"Let's go! Full speed ahead!" I call.
"We'll break the record, Cannonball!"

But something's wrong! We hear a crack!
Another train is on the track!
Casey brakes. We see a flash!
He slows me down. Too late!

WE CRASH!

Casey's braking saved his crew.
It saved his many riders, too.
But Casey Jones, he stayed inside.
He wouldn't jump,
And so he died.

We were the greatest team of all—
Casey Jones and Cannonball.
And year by year our legend grew.
You read to me, I'll read to you.

The End

We're done with short.

        We're done with tall.

We've read them each.

        We've read them all.

The tall tales stretch
From sea to sea.

        They tell of how
        Things came to be.

They tell of ships

        And daring deeds,

Of grizzly bears

        And apple seeds.

And every hero
In each story

        Found a way
        To gain some glory,

Shooting sharp
Or fighting strong,

        Sometimes remembered
        In a song.

No one made
A lot of money

        But they had fun
        And they were funny.

They were brave

        And they were clever;

        And their names
        Will live forever.